123
SESAME STREET®

W9-CHM-583

S is for School!

By P.J. Shaw
Illustrated by Tom Brannon

Dalmatian Press, LLC, 2011. All rights reserved.
Published by Dalmatian Press, LLC, 2011. The DALMATIAN PRESS name and logo are trademarks of Dalmatian Press, LLC, Franklin, Tennessee 37067. No part of this book may be reproduced or copied in any form without written permission from the copyright owner.

Printed in Haining,
Zhejiang, China

CE13862

Hello, Dorothy! Today was Elmo's first day of school. What's that, Dorothy? You want to know what it's like on the very first day of school? Elmo will tell you.

The first day of school is *so* exciting!

Just getting there is an adventure!

Some monsters wonder what to do on the first day of school.

So it helps to have a buddy.

Furry ones are fun!

At school, you might feel a little lonely now and then.

But a smile helps you make new friends.
A smile—and some crayons!

On the first day of school, a little fish can get homesick... so bring a picture for company. Guess what? Elmo brings a picture of Dorothy!

On the first day of school
you see lots of new faces.

Lots of *friendly* faces! Yay!

The *end* of the first day of school is exciting, too.

It's a good time
for sharing what you've learned...

...with a friend!